USBORNE

GREEK
MYTHS

USBORNE HOTSHOTS

GREEK MYTHS

Cheryl Evans and Judy Tatchell

Designed by Heather Blackham
Edited by Lisa Miles

Illustrated by Rodney Matthews,
Ian Jackson and Nick Harris

Consultant: Anne Millard

Series designer: Ruth Russell

CONTENTS

4 The Ancient Greeks

5 The Creation

6 Zeus' revenge

7 The gods' family tree

8 What the gods were like

10 Bellerophon and the Chimaera

12 Perseus and Medusa

14 Jason and the Golden Fleece

16 Theseus and the Minotaur

20 Heracles and the Twelve Labours

24 Helen and Paris

26 The Trojan War

28 The adventures of Odysseus

30 More myths

32 Index

The Ancient Greeks

Greek history can be traced back 40,000 years but the best-known period is called the Classical Period (500-336BC). The versions of Greek myths passed down to us often date from stories and plays written in and after that period. At that time, the land that we now call Greece, and the west coast of Turkey, was divided into many small states. The most important ones are shown on the map on the right.

Hermes became the god of thieves because he once stole cattle from the sun god, Apollo.

About the gods

The Greek gods behaved rather like the Ancient Greeks did themselves. They got married, had children, argued and had human failings such as jealousy. They even fell in love with humans and many Greek myths feature people as well as gods.

Bronze statue of a monster called a Chimaera.

What are the Greek myths?

The myths formed part of the religion of Ancient Greece. This featured many gods and goddesses, each responsible for some aspect of everyday life. People prayed to whichever ones were most relevant to them at the time. Some myths are about heroes. These may actually be based on real people, though much changed.

In each story in this book you will find a box with the title *How to say...* The box tells you how to pronounce the names of the characters and places that feature in that story. See the box on the opposite page for an example. You need to emphasize the part of the name shown in **bold** type.

4

The Creation

The world forms.

The Ancient Greek religion tried to explain how the world began. The story was that before the world existed, there was a dark nothingness, called Chaos. Gradually, the shape of Mother Earth, or Gaea, emerged from the emptiness and formed the world. She gave birth to a son, Uranus, who was the Sky. Rain fell from the Sky causing plants to grow. Animals then appeared from the rivers and seas.

Monsters and giants

Next, monsters and giants were born. Among these were three giants who each had only one huge eye in the middle of their foreheads. They were called Cyclopes, meaning "wheel-eyed". Uranus treated the Cyclopes cruelly and banished them to the Underworld, where people went when they died. Later, human-shaped giants called Titans were born. These were the first gods and goddesses.

A Cyclops.

The first gods

Mother Earth was furious with Uranus for treating the Cyclopes so cruelly. She urged the Titan leader, Cronos, to rebel and seize power. Cronos attacked Uranus, and a drop of Uranus' blood fell in the sea, making foam from which Aphrodite, the goddess of love, was born.

Father swallows children

Cronos married his sister Rhea and became the Titan King. They had five children but Cronos had been warned one of them would kill him, so he swallowed each child as it was born. To save the sixth, Rhea tricked

Nymphs

Cronos into swallowing a stone wrapped in baby's clothes instead. She gave the real baby to some nymphs to bring up. This child was Zeus.

How to say...

Aphrodite: aff-ro-*die*-tee
Chaos: kay-oss
Cronos: kron-oss
Cyclopes: sye-klo-peas
Rhea: ree-a
Titans: tie-tans
Uranus: you-rain-uss
Zeus: zyooss

Zeus' revenge

Silver coin showing Zeus.

When Zeus grew up, he returned home in disguise and gave Cronos a potion to make him choke. His brothers and sisters were coughed out, whole and safe.

Eventually, Zeus won, married his sister Hera and became Ruler of the Sky and King of the Gods. Poseidon became King of the Ocean, and Pluto King of the Underworld.

The last battle

Then, there was a fierce battle between Zeus and the Titans. Zeus freed the Cyclopes who made thunderbolts for him to hurl, a trident for Poseidon, and a helmet for Pluto which made him invisible.

Statue of the god Poseidon.

The gods' family tree

This family tree shows the relationships between the most important Greek gods. The gods were immortal and had supernatural powers such as the ability to change shape. They lived on top of Mount Olympus, a high mountain in northern Greece. The gods whose names are in capital letters are described over the page.

> **Key to family tree**
> • • • married
> ——— gave birth to

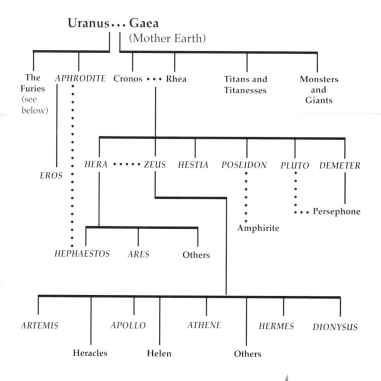

Uranus • • • Gaea (Mother Earth)

- The Furies (see below)
- APHRODITE
- Cronos • • • Rhea
- Titans and Titanesses
- Monsters and Giants

EROS

HERA • • • • • ZEUS   HESTIA   POSEIDON   PLUTO   DEMETER

• • • Persephone

Amphirite

HEPHAESTOS   ARES   Others

ARTEMIS   APOLLO   ATHENE   HERMES   DIONYSUS

Heracles   Helen   Others

The three Furies were appointed by the gods to make murderers, especially those who killed relatives, feel unbearably guilty. They tormented a victim until the sin was avenged. They had dogs' heads, snakes for hair and bats' wings.

What the gods were like

Zeus (zyoos)

Ruler of the gods. Married to Hera but frequently unfaithful. Appeared in many disguises. Domineering and powerful, terrifying when angry.

Hera (hair-a)

Queen of the gods, sister and wife of Zeus. Protector of marriage and women. Beautiful and proud, often persecuted Zeus' lovers and their children. The peacock was her symbol.

Athene (a-thee-nee)

Goddess of wisdom and war, patron of Athens. Dangerous if roused to anger. Always wore armour. Unbeatable in combat.

Hestia (hess-tee-a)

Goddess of the hearth, protector of the home. Gentle, aloof from quarrels of other gods. Resigned throne, knowing she would be welcomed on Earth.

Pluto (ploo-toe)

Ruler of the Underworld, the Kingdom of the Dead. Rich – owned all precious metals and jewels. Gloomy and frightening. Had helmet of invisibility.

Poseidon (poss-eye-don)

Ruled the seas from an underwater palace. Controlled storms and sea monsters. Caused earthquakes – known as the earth-shaker.

Ares (are-eez)

God of war. Strong and handsome. Aphrodite's lover. Short-tempered and violent, might intervene on opposing sides, indifferent to rights and wrongs.

Apollo (a-poll-o)

God of sun, light, truth, music, poetry, science and healing. His priestesses could foretell the future. Artistic, could be cruel.

Hephaestos (heff-eest-os)

Lame, employed by the gods in their forge – admired for his work. Suffered wife Aphrodite's infidelities. Could make supernaturally powerful weapons.

Aphrodite (aff-ro-die-tee)

Goddess of love and beauty. Married to Hephaestos. Had a magic golden belt which made her irresistible. Charming but fickle and vain.

Artemis (are-tem-iss)

Moon goddess. Protector of animals, children and pregnant women. Loved hunting (was a perfect shot). Independent, merciless.

Demeter (de-meet-a)

Goddess of plants and harvests, responsible for growth and fertility of crops. Generous and bountiful, with a strong maternal instinct.

Eros (ee-ross)

Son of Aphrodite and an unknown father. Charming, young and handsome, he made people fall in love with each other by shooting them with his golden bow and arrows. Mischievous.

Hermes (her-meez)

Messenger of the gods, god of travellers and thieves. Had a winged helmet and sandals. Quick-witted, mischievous.

Dionysus (die-on-eye-sus)

God of wine. Went around teaching people how to make wine, accompanied by wild followers. Took Hestia's place amongst the gods on Mount Olympus.

Bellerophon and the Chimaera

Many of the Greek myths involve fabulous creatures and terrible monsters. In this story, a young man whose name was Bellerophon uses the winged horse, Pegasus, to slay a lethal beast, the Chimaera.

Falsely accused

Bellerophon lived in the court of Proteus, King of Argos in Greece. He was wrongly accused of trying to seduce King Proteus' wife.

How to say...

Bellerophon: bell-air-oh-fon
Chimaera: kim-ear-a
Lycia: lissy-a
Metis: mee-tiss
Pegasus: peg-a-suss
Proteus: pro-tee-us

Poison pen letter

In revenge, Proteus sent Bellerophon to the King of Lycia with a letter. Unknown to Bellerophon, the letter asked the king to kill the person who delivered it. The king, though, did not want to risk offending the Furies by killing his guest. Instead, he asked Bellerophon to kill the Chimaera in return for his hospitality. The king was sure Bellerophon would fail and be killed himself.

Gift of the goddess

The goddess Athene decided to help Bellerophon. She lent him her winged horse, Pegasus. On Pegasus' back, Bellerophon flew over the Chimaera and plunged a spear deep into its throat.

The Chimaera had a lion's head, a goat's body and a serpent's tail. It breathed fire.

Pegasus was loyal to any master. Zeus used him to carry his thunderbolts.

Secret weapon

Bellerophon then used Pegasus to help the King of Lycia overcome his enemies, by flying above their armies and pelting them with rocks. The king could not believe the hero deserved to die after such a show of loyalty, and they became friends. Bellerophon even married the king's daughter.

A bad end

Bellerophon became proud, though. He flew to Mount Olympus on Pegasus. No human was allowed in the home of the gods without an invitation, so Zeus punished him. He sent a fly that drove Pegasus wild. Bellerophon was thrown and landed in a thorn bush. Blinded and lame, he ended his life homeless and alone.

The birth of Athene

Metis, a Titaness, was expecting Zeus' baby when he was warned that the child would be greater than him. So he turned Metis into a fly and swallowed her. Later, Zeus had a terrible headache and ordered the blacksmith god, Hephaestos, to crack open his head. Hephaestos did so, knowing that he could not harm an immortal god. From the split appeared Athene, fully armed.

The owl was Athene's special symbol.

11

Perseus and Medusa

Perseus and his mother, Danae, lived on the island of Seriphos. Polydictes, the King of Seriphos, wanted Danae to marry him, but she refused. Polydictes thought she might change her mind if Perseus went away, so he sent the young man off to kill the monster Medusa, to prove his courage.

Medusa, daughter of a sea god, offended Athene who turned her into a monster.

The gods lend a hand

Anyone who looked at Medusa's frightful face was turned to stone. As it was Athene who had created this monster, she decided to help Perseus kill her. Athene gave Perseus a shiny shield and told him to look only at Medusa's reflection, not directly at her. Hermes gave Perseus a sickle and Pluto lent him his helmet of invisibility. They also gave him a magic bag and winged sandals.

How to say...

Acrisius: a-krees-yus
Andromeda: an-drom-med-a
Danae: dan-eye
Medusa: med-ewe-sah
Perseus: per-syoos
Polydictes: polly-dic-tees
Seriphos: serr-y-fos

Monster is slain

Perseus found Medusa, and used his magic weapons to cut off her head. He put the head in the bag and escaped on his winged sandals. Flying home, he saw a beautiful princess called Andromeda chained to a rock, and fell in love with her.

A human sacrifice

Andromeda's parents had offended Poseidon who had flooded their land as a punishment. To appease him, Andromeda was to be sacrificed to a sea monster. As the monster approached her, Perseus sprang out and killed it. Then he freed the princess and married her. When they returned to Seriphos, King Polydictes was about to force Danae into marriage. Outraged, Perseus held up Medusa's head, Polydictes looked at it and was instantly turned to stone.

The birth of Perseus

Perseus' parents were Danae and Zeus. Danae's father, King Acrisius, had been warned that he would be killed by his grandson.

He locked his daughter away so that she could never have children. He could not keep her from Zeus, though. The King of the gods had the power to change into many forms, and entered Danae's prison as a shower of gold.

Zeus comes to Danae.

When Perseus was born, Acrisius could not bear to kill him, so he set him adrift in a boat with his mother. Zeus guided the boat safely to the island of Seriphos.

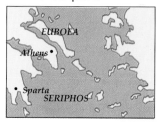

Jason and the Golden Fleece

Jason was heir to the kingdom of Iolcus but his uncle Pelias stole the crown when Jason was a baby. Jason and his deposed father were banished but when Jason grew up, he returned to claim his crown. Pelias said Jason could be heir if he brought back the sacred Golden Fleece from Colchis. He did not expect Jason to return. Jason built a great ship, the Argo, and gathered a crew of heroes, known as the Argonauts.

The Argo

A shipful of heroes

On the way, they had to pass between the Clashing Rocks, which crashed shut and crushed anything trying to pass. They sent a bird through to make the rocks shut. As they reopened, the heroes rowed quickly through before the rocks could shut again.

Orpheus

How to say...

Aeetes: ee-ee-tees
Argonauts: are-go-norts
Capri: ka-pree
Colchis: kol-kis
Iolcus: ee-ol-kus
Jason: jay-son
Medea: med-ee-a
Orpheus: or-fee-us
Pelias: pee-lee-ass

A witch's magic

The King of Colchis, Aeetes, had no intention of letting Jason have the fleece. He set him a task which he was sure would kill him. Jason had to harness two fire-breathing bulls, plough a field with them and plant it with dragons' teeth. The gods made Aeetes' daughter, the witch Medea, fall in love with Jason and help him. Medea gave Jason a potion to protect him from the bulls' breath. As he planted the teeth, vicious soldiers sprang up. On Medea's advice, Jason threw a stone among them. One soldier thought another had attacked him, fighting broke out, and they all killed each other.

The monster sleeps

The fleece was guarded by a fearsome dragon which was never known to sleep. One of the Argonauts, Orpheus, was a great musician. On Medea's advice, Orpheus played a lullaby until the monster finally closed its eyes. Jason grabbed the fleece and ran to the Argo with Medea, swearing to marry her and always be faithful.

The Golden Fleece came from a sacred ram which had been sent by Hera to rescue two children, Phrixus and Helle, from their scheming stepmother Ino.

The song of the sirens

Sailing home, they passed Capri. There they heard the beautiful singing of sea nymphs, called sirens, which lured sailors to their deaths on the rocks. Orpheus played his lyre to drown their voices, and the Argo passed safely.

Jason takes the crown

Back in Iolcus, Medea tricked Pelias' daughters into killing him, saying they could restore his youth by boiling him in a cauldron. The crown was then free for Jason.

A hero's decline

The people were sickened by Medea's cruelty, and banished them both. They went to Corinth, where Jason became king. He ruled well at first, but became arrogant and broke his promise to be faithful to Medea. The gods became angry and made Jason an outcast.

He wandered until he found the rotting hull of the Argo. As he sat dreaming of the past, the prow of the old ship crashed down and killed him – a warning to anyone who broke his oath.

Theseus and the Minotaur

The son of Minos, King of Crete, had been killed in Athens. In compensation Minos demanded that fourteen young Athenians be sent to Crete every nine years to be fed to the Minotaur. This was a terrible monster, half-man, half-bull, which fed on human flesh. It lived in a maze called the Labyrinth. No one who went in ever came out alive.

A hero sets sail

Theseus lived in the court of King Aegeus of Athens. Both Aegeus and the god Poseidon had loved Theseus' mother and either could have been his father, but Aegeus believed Theseus was his heir. Theseus said he would kill the Minotaur. Aegeus was afraid for his son. He asked the sailors to hoist white sails on their return, instead of the usual black, if Theseus was still alive.

A tough test

In Crete, Minos dared Theseus to prove whether Poseidon was his father, by retrieving a ring thrown into the sea. Theseus dived, praying to Poseidon for help. Some sea goddesses found the ring for him and he emerged in triumph.

Into the maze

Minos' daughter Ariadne fell in love with Theseus and offered to help him if he would promise to marry her. He agreed, and she gave him a magic ball of twine. When he entered the Labyrinth, he tied one end to the entrance, then followed as it unwound and led him to the bull-like Minotaur, lurking deep in the maze. After a terrible fight, Theseus overcame the Minotaur and followed the magic twine out of the Labyrinth.

Minos' mother

Princess Europa was on a beach when Zeus appeared as a white bull. The gentle bull carried her off to Crete. There she had three sons with Zeus. Later she married the King of Crete who made her eldest son, Minos, his heir.

The bull was so gentle that Europa climbed on its back for a ride.

How to say...

Aegeus: ij-ee-us
Ariadne: arry-ad-nee
Labyrinth: lab-ber-inth
Minos: my-noss
Minotaur: my-no-tore
Theseus: thee-syoos

The great escape!

Theseus escaped with Ariadne by boat. They stopped at the island of Naxos, where Ariadne slept. Ungrateful Theseus sailed off without her, despite his promise to marry her. When she woke, she cried to the gods for revenge.

Ariadne's revenge

The god Dionysus passed the island and fell in love with Ariadne. They married and Dionysus granted her revenge by making Theseus forget to hoist white sails as he returned to Athens. When Aegeus saw the black sails on the distant ship, he thought his son was dead and jumped into the sea, drowning himself in despair. The sea where he died is called the Aegean Sea after him.

Theseus and Aridne escape.

What became of Theseus

In these sad circumstances, Theseus became King of Athens in his father's place. Theseus married Hippolyta, an Amazon queen. She later died fighting at Theseus' side in battle. Their son, Hippolytus, was killed through the wickedness and jealousy of Theseus' second wife, Phaedra.

After these tragic deaths, Theseus went adventuring again. He eventually settled on the island of Skyros and died there. His love for Athens, though, outlasted his death. Hundreds of years later, when the city was about to lose the Battle of Marathon in 490BC, Theseus' ghost appeared to inspire the troops and led them to victory over the Persians. After that, his body was brought home to Athens and buried there with honours.

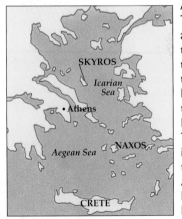

The Labyrinth maker

Daedalus, an inventor, was imprisoned with his son Icarus, for offending King Minos. Minos forced Daedalus to design the Minotaur's fiendish Labyrinth.

Father and son eventually escaped on wings they had made of feathers and wax. Icarus disobeyed his father and flew so high that the sun melted the wax. The wings came apart and Icarus fell into the sea, later known as the Icarian Sea.

Icarus

How to say...

Daedalus: deed-a-lus
Hippolyta:
 hip-poll-itta
Hippolytus:
 hip-poll-ittus
Icarus: ick-er-us
Naxos: nack-soss
Skyros: sky-ross
Semele:
 sem-a-lee
Silenus:
 sye-lee-nus

More about the Minotaur

Crete often suffered from earthquakes. The myth of the bull-like Minotaur may have come about to explain the way the ground rumbled and shook. Bulls were sacred in Cretan culture. The wall-painting above shows a ritual called bull-leaping.

Dionysus, the merry god

Dionysus' mother was a Theban princess called Semele, who died before he was born. Dionysus, though, was kept safe in the thigh of his father, Zeus, until his birth.

Dionysus was brought up by a fun-loving half-god called Silenus and the pair roamed the world, making merry. They knew the secret of making wine from grapes and they taught people the skill wherever they went.

Dionysus

19

Heracles and the Twelve Labours

Heracles was the son of Zeus and Alcmene. When he was born, Zeus' wife Hera was so infuriated that she sent two deadly serpents to the baby's cradle. Heracles strangled them both, stunning everyone with his incredible strength.

Madness brings tragedy

Years later, Heracles married a woman named Megara and they had a family. Hera was jealous of his happiness and drove him mad. In his madness, Heracles killed his wife and children. When he recovered and realized what he had done, he was devastated.

Heracles asked the gods how he could make amends. He was given twelve terrible tasks, or labours. If he completed them all, he would be rid of his guilt, and become a god.

The next three pages describe the twelve labours of Heracles.

How to say...

Alcmene: alk-mee-nee
Augean: awe-jee-an
Ceryneian: sair-ee-nee-an
Heracles: hair-a-kleez
Lernaean Hydra: ler-nee-an hide-ra
Megara: meg-er-a
Nemean: neem-ee-an
Stymphalian: stim-fail-ee-an

Heracles and the Nemean lion

1. Kill the Nemean lion

The Nemean lion's hide was so tough, no weapon could pierce it. Heracles had to strangle it with his bare hands. Afterwards, he wore the lion's skin for protection.

Silver coin showing Heracles

2. Destroy the Lernaean Hydra

The Hydra of Lerna had a dog's body and nine serpents' heads, which grew right back if they were cut off. Heracles had to sever the heads and seal the necks with a torch to kill the beast.

3. Capture the Ceryneian hind

The Ceryneian hind was a deer with bronze hooves and golden horns.

The Ceryneian hind was sacred to Artemis, the goddess of hunting. Heracles stalked it for a year before he was able to catch it in a net.

4. Trap the Erymanthian boar

The Erymanthian boar was an enormous, fierce creature which filled people with terror. To capture it, Heracles hunted the beast and drove it into a deep snowdrift. While it was floundering, he quickly bound it with chains.

5. Clean the Augean stables in a day

King Augeus' stables had not been cleaned for many years and they were piled high with dung. Heracles diverted a nearby river so that it swept through the stables and washed the muck away.

6. Destroy the Stymphalian birds

The Stymphalian birds had bronze beaks, claws and wings.

These vicious birds had bronze beaks, claws and wings, and ate human flesh. To destroy them, Heracles startled them into flight, and then shot their soft bodies with his arrows.

Heracles and the Twelve Labours (continued)

7. Capture the Cretan bull

This huge, untamed bull, which caused havoc as it rampaged through Crete, was the father of the Minotaur (see page 16). Heracles managed to master the animal and carried it off by boat.

8. Round up the mares of Diomedes

These wild horses fed on human flesh. Heracles killed their master, Diomedes, and fed him to the mares. When they had eaten, they were calmer, and Heracles managed to control them.

Taming the wild horses of Diomedes.

9. Bring Hippolyta's girdle

Hippolyta was queen of the Amazons, a fierce race of warrior women. Hippolyta was happy to give Heracles her girdle, or belt, but Hera made the other Amazons think he was hurting her. They attacked and he had to fight the whole army to get the girdle.

10. Bring the cattle of Geryon

These cattle were guarded by a two-headed dog and Geryon, a man with three bodies above the waist. Heracles killed them. He then set up two pillars to guard the Mediterranean Sea.

11. Bring the golden apples of the Hesperides

The Hesperides were daughters of Atlas, who had been ordered by Zeus to carry the heavens. Atlas agreed to bring back the apples if Heracles would take his place as he did so. When he returned, Atlas refused to take back his burden. Heracles agreed to stay but asked Atlas to take the weight for a moment so he could settle more comfortably. Atlas did so, and Heracles escaped with the apples.

12. Bring Cerberus from the underworld

Cerberus was a three-headed dog who guarded the gates of the Underworld. Pluto said Heracles could take Cerberus as long as he used no weapons. Heracles dragged the dog away.

How to say...

Cerberus: *sir-ber-us*
Diomedes: *die-om-ee-deez*
Geryon: *gair-eye-on*

The death of Heracles

Heracles later married again and had several children, but Hera had her final revenge and eventually caused his death. She tricked his new wife into giving Heracles a magic robe to keep him faithful. In fact the robe was poisoned. It caused him agony, but he could not remove it.

Peace at last

Heracles built a funeral pyre and climbed onto it to die in the flames and escape the pain at last. Suddenly, Zeus appeared and snatched his son from the fire. He took him to the god's home on Mount Olympus, where Heracles became a god.

Helen and Paris

Paris chooses Aphrodite.

Thetis and Peleus were to be married. Eris, the goddess of spite, was furious at not being invited to the wedding, and decided to take revenge.

The apple of strife

She took an apple to the feast, inscribed *For the fairest*. Hera, Athene and Aphrodite all reached for it. Zeus did not want to be the judge, imagining the fury of the two not chosen. He decided Paris, prince of Troy, should choose.

How to say...

*Cassandra: cass-**and**-ra*
*Eris: **air**-iss*
*Menelaus: men-a-**lay**-us*
*Odysseus: oh-**dee**-see-us*
*Peleus: **pee**-lyoos*
*Priam: **pry**-am*
*Thetis: **thee**-tiss*
*Uranus: **you**-rain-us*

Paris has to choose

Paris was on a hillside when Hermes arrived with the goddesses. Each tried to bribe Paris. Hera offered power and wealth. Athene offered great victories and wisdom. Aphrodite, the goddess of love, promised Paris that if he chose her, the most beautiful woman in the world would fall in love with him. Paris could not resist Aphrodite and chose her.

Paris goes to Greece

Earlier, the Greeks had kidnapped the sister of Paris' father, King Priam of Troy. Priam sent Paris to arrange her release. If the Greeks would not let her go, Paris was instructed to seize a Greek princess in return.

A husband for Helen

Helen was the wife of King Menelaus, in Greece. She was the most beautiful woman in the world and many men had wanted to marry her. Before choosing a husband for her, Helen's foster father had made all the suitors promise to support the chosen man. They agreed, and he chose Menelaus.

Helen falls in love

Helen had never loved Menelaus and when Paris arrived from Troy she fell in love with him, as Aphrodite had promised. She agreed to go back to Troy with him, so the Trojans went home with a Greek princess as planned. Menelaus was furious. He asked his brother and all Helen's former suitors to help him fetch her back.

An unwilling army

Many of the suitors did not want to go to war, despite their promise of support. One of them, Odysseus, pretended to be insane and started to plough the beach when Menelaus' men came for him. But they placed his baby son in his path, and Odysseus swerved to avoid him, proving that he was sane.

A prediction ignored

Helen had charmed the Trojans but Paris' sister, Cassandra, predicted the war would end in disaster for Troy. Cassandra had displeased Apollo, who had put a curse on her so that nobody ever believed her predictions.

A thousand Greek ships prepared to sail to Troy. The Trojan War, Eris' spiteful revenge, began.

More about Aphrodite

Aphrodite was the goddess of love. When Uranus was defeated by Zeus (see page 5), a drop of his blood fell into the ocean. From the foam, Aphrodite appeared. She was carried to Cyprus on a giant scallop shell, and given clothes and jewels by the Seasons. Doves and sparrows flocked around her, and became her special birds.

Aphrodite appears.

The Trojan War

The Trojan War went on for ten years. The Greeks could not break into Troy, and the Trojans could not drive them off.

Greek soldiers camped outside the city of Troy during the siege.

The greatest warrior

The most famous Greek warrior was Achilles, one of the seven sons of Thetis and Peleus. Thetis had made the other six immortal by burning away their mortal half. She was doing the same for the baby Achilles when Peleus stopped her, thinking she was hurting the child. Achilles was left with one vulnerable place on his body where he could be fatally wounded – the heel by which Thetis had held him.

The strain begins to show

The war dragged on and tempers began to fray. Achilles argued with King Agamemnon, the Greek leader, and left the battle, sulking. The Greeks lost heart and were driven back by the Trojan prince, Hector. In desperation, Achilles' friend, Patroclus, put on Achilles' armour and led an attack, but he was not as skilled as Achilles and Hector killed him.

Death after death

Achilles was stricken by guilt. He killed Hector and dragged his body around the city behind his chariot. Paris avenged Hector's death by shooting Achilles in his vulnerable heel, and killing him. Eventually, Paris was killed by a crack shot from a Greek archer called Philoctetes. This gave the Greeks new hope.

A cunning trick

Troy finally fell thanks to a trick thought up by Odysseus. The Greeks pretended to give up. Then they built a huge wooden horse as a gift to Athene, left it outside Troy and sailed away. The Trojans were overjoyed. They pulled the horse into the city and began to celebrate.

> ### How to say...
>
> *Achilles: a-kill-eez*
> *Agamemnon: ag-a-mem-non*
> *Patroclus: pat-rock-luss*
> *Philoctetes: fill-lock-tee-tees*

The city falls

That night as the Trojans slept, some Greeks who had hidden inside the hollow horse crept out. They opened the city gates to let in the Greek army who had sneaked back under cover of darkness. The Greeks destroyed the city and recaptured Helen. At last, the war was over.

A picture of the wooden horse taken from a Greek vase.

The adventures of Odysseus

After the Trojan War, Odysseus' journey home was full of mishaps. On one island where they stopped for supplies, a Cyclops shut Odysseus and his men in a cave with his sheep and began to eat them one by one.

Odysseus blinded the one-eyed giant with a stick while he slept. Next day, when the sheep were let out to graze, the men clung to their bellies. The blind Cyclops felt each sheep to make sure the men were not escaping, but he did not feel underneath them, so the sailors got away.

A helping hand

The gods helped Odysseus by giving him the storm winds in a bag, but his greedy men opened it, looking for treasure. They released a terrible storm which drove the ship to the home of the witch Circe.

A witch's hospitality

Circe turned Odysseus' men into pigs but Hermes gave Odysseus a flower to make him immune to Circe's spells. Circe fell in love with him and restored his men.

How to say...

Charybdis: kar-rib-diss
Circe: seer-see
Cyclops: sye-klops
Penelope: pen-ell-oh-pee
Scylla: sill-a

An awful choice

Odysseus stayed with Circe and they had three sons but still Odysseus wanted to go home. When he and his men finally left, they had to sail through a narrow channel between two monsters. One was Scylla, who had six heads and snapping dogs at her waist. The other was a deadly whirlpool, Charybdis. Odysseus decided to sail closer to Scylla and they just got by, though some of his men were killed.

Trouble at home

At last Odysseus reached Ithaca and entered his court disguised as an old man. He found noblemen squandering his wealth and trying to make his wife Penelope marry one of them, saying Odysseus must be dead. Poor Penelope kept delaying her decision, saying she must finish her weaving first. She wove by day and then undid her work at night, until her trick was discovered.

A bloody revenge

Odysseus revealed his identity to his son and they secretly hid all the nobles' weapons. Penelope said she would marry the man who could string a bow Odysseus had left behind. She was sure the nobles would fail, and they did. Then Odysseus took up the bow, strung it easily and shot an arrow. Realizing who he must be, the nobles reached for their weapons, but they were gone. Odysseus had no pity and killed them all.

More myths

Prometheus

Zeus asked Prometheus, a Titan, to try his hand at creating a race to live on Earth. Prometheus succeeded by making mankind. He made them in the image of the gods themselves. Prometheus was very fond of the people he had created and helped them whenever he could.

He felt sorry for mankind. With the help of Athene, his friend, he stole some fire from Zeus' palace and showed people how to use it.

The eagle swoops.

Zeus' punishment

When Zeus found out, he chained Prometheus to a rock and made an eagle eat his liver. Despite the pain, the immortal Prometheus could not die. His liver grew at night and the eagle returned the next day. Many centuries later, Zeus allowed Prometheus to be rescued by Heracles.

Pandora

Zeus punished mankind for accepting Prometheus' gift of fire. He asked Hephaestos to shape a woman in his forge.

Zeus then breathed life into her and sent her to Prometheus' brother, Epimetheus. Zeus gave her a jar to take with her but strictly forbade her to open it.

Pandora is often said to have had a box, but "jar" is another translation of the Greek word.

Epimetheus married the woman, called Pandora. She was very lovely, but could not resist peeping inside Zeus' jar.

Out of the jar flew all the evils that plague the world – sickness, age, sin and death. As Pandora stared in horror, one last thing emerged – Hope. This meant that people should never be in despair.

King Midas

The god Dionysus was grateful to King Midas for looking after Silenus, who had brought him up. To thank him, Dionysus granted Midas a wish.

A wish for gold

The greedy king asked that everything he touched should turn to gold. He soon regretted this when his daughter turned into a gold statue and even his food turned to gold. He pleaded with Dionysus to undo the wish, which he did.

Everything King Midas touched turned to gold.

Echo and Narcissus

The nymph Echo had offended Hera. As a punishment, Hera condemned her never to say anything of her own again. Echo could only ever repeat other people's last words.

Echo fell in love with Narcissus. He was handsome, but vain and hard-hearted. Following him, she endlessly repeated his words, until she faded away with sorrow, leaving only her voice.

Self-love

Narcissus made many other lovers unhappy, until Artemis decided to punish him. She showed him his own reflection in a pool and he fell deeply in love with it. When he realized he would never love anyone else as much, he stabbed himself to death in despair.

The flower called narcissus sprang up from his blood.

31

Index

Achilles 26
Aegeus, King of Athens 16-18
Amphirite 7
Andromeda 13
Aphrodite 5, 7, 9, 24-25
  birth 25
Apollo 4, 7, 9, 25
Ares 7, 8
Ariadne 16-18
Argonauts 14-15
Artemis 7, 9, 21, 31
Athene 7, 8, 10, 12, 24, 26, 30
  birth 11
Athens 8, 16, 18
Atlas 22

Bellerophon 10-11

Chaos 5
Charybdis 29
Chimaera 4, 10-11
Circe 28-29
Crete 16, 19, 22
Cronos 5, 6, 7
Cyclopes 5, 6, 28

Daedalus 19
Demeter 7, 9
Dionysus 7, 9, 18, 19, 31

Echo 31
Eris 24, 25
Eros 7, 9
Europa 16

Furies 7

Golden Fleece 14

Hector 26
Helen 7, 24-25, 27
Hephaestos 7, 9, 30
Hera 7, 8, 15, 20, 23, 24, 31
Heracles 7, 20-23, 30
Hermes 4, 7, 9
Hestia 7, 8
Hippolyta 18, 22
Hippolytus 18

Icarus 19

Jason 14-15

Marathon, battle of 18
Medusa 12-13
Menelaus, King 25
Midas, King 31
Minotaur 16-17, 19, 22
Mother Earth (Gaea) 5, 7
monsters 7, 10
Mount Olympus 7, 11, 23
Narcissus 31

Odysseus 25, 26, 28-29
Orpheus 14

Pandora 30
Paris 24-25, 26
Pegasus 10-11
Persephone 7
Perseus 12-13
Pluto 6, 7, 8
Poseidon 6, 7, 8, 13
Prometheus 30

Rhea 5, 7

Scylla 29
Silenus 19, 31
sirens 15

Theseus 16-18
Titans 5, 6, 7
Trojan War 25, 26-27, 28
Troy 24, 25, 26
twelve labours 20-23

Uranus 5, 7, 25

wooden horse 26-27

Zeus 5, 6, 7, 8, 11, 13, 19, 20
  and Aphrodite 25
  and Heracles 23
  and Pandora 30
  and Prometheus 30

Additional illustrations by: Joe McEwan (5, middle; 6, top, 19, middle), Jan Nesbitt (5, bottom).

This book is based on material previously published in *The Usborne Illustrated Guide to Greek Myths and Legends* and *The Usborne Illustrated World History: The Greeks.*

First published in 1995 by Usborne Publishing Ltd, Usborne House, 83-85 Saffron Hill, London EC1N 8RT, England.

Copyright © Usborne Publishing Ltd 1986, 1990, 1995.